25 TRUMBULLS ROAD

25 TRUMBULLS ROAD

CHRISTOPHER LOCKE

Black
Lawrence
Press

www.blacklawrence.com

Executive Editor: Diane Goettel
Chapbook Editor: Kit Frick
Book and Cover Design: Amy Freels

Copyright © Christopher Locke 2020
ISBN: 978-1-62557-715-3

Published 2020 by Black Lawrence Press.
Printed in the United States.

For George Heath Locke:
the first storyteller to hold me spellbound.

Contents

CASE 3

(August 2000)

EXHIBIT #1 The first night in our new house, I had a dream about a woman who lived under the floor. She smelled raw and cried as she pulled her body between the wide pine planks. I wanted to help her but felt that would be rude somehow. She quieted when she took me outside the house, which miraculously looked exactly like the one we just moved into; our real cars were in the driveway, my real cat was silhouetted in the upstairs window, licking its paw. She brought me into the nearby woods and seated me atop a stump. I watched as she shuffled around a great, gnarled apple tree, humming, dragging her damaged feet. She stopped abruptly and turned toward me, opening her mouth wide. When I woke up, I felt unusual, almost heartsick. The morning was glorious, and my daughter Sophie asked me to join her outside after breakfast to explore our new neighborhood. We went into the woods, discovered an abandoned doll house with three little beds, each bed holding only the head of a doll, nothing more. We kept going, pushing at brambles and dead pine, until we happened upon an apple tree. Around the base of the tree was a muddy, worn path. I felt the blood leave my face, and I could hear music not far off.

EXHIBIT #4 The woman who lives under the floor came back last night. She was standing in my bedroom doorway, resplendent in a bright wedding gown. But it also seemed like she'd been crying, and when I looked closer, I could tell that she was rain-soaked, several brown oak leaves matted against her hem. I followed her downstairs, and each time she stepped forward all the doors in the house slammed. When she lifted her foot, they opened. I was close enough behind to see her shoulder blades pushing softly up through the lace. She smelled like coal dust and cardamom. She brought me to the kitchen. Everything, again, was as clear as it is in the normal world: the little microwave clock glowed 3:03 a.m.; the dishtowel embroidered with a purple lilac hung on the oven door handle exactly as I placed it before going to bed. I asked her to go outside, away from this house. She turned around and stepped toward me. SLAM went the doors. I stepped back. She raised her naked foot, and the doors opened, like taking a breath. She stepped down. SLAM. She opened her mouth, and I could hear night clicking around me like an insect. That's when I woke up. My left foot was aching; deep cramp. I sat up slowly, grimacing, letting the comforter fall to the floor. Outside, the wind was rapacious; a pile of dead leaves geysered up from the yard, and a row of little plum trees bowed like the condemned before they're led away.

EXHIBIT #5 *Redacted.*

EXHIBIT #7 Planting bulbs, Sophie and my husband work their way around the house to the south side. There, under about five inches of black soil, they discover the bodies of three antique dolls, the kind that can shatter if dropped. All three are missing their heads. The dolls are each dressed in what look like silk gowns, white, and appear to not have been buried long. We have no idea why these are here or who put them underground. "There they are," says Sophie. "There are what," my husband wants to know. "My doll shoes. They went missing after we moved in." Sure enough, each headless little body is wearing a pair of patent leather shoes from Sophie's extensive collection. My husband looks at me funny, and I can tell he's afraid. That night, I get up out of bed and crouch on the floor. I put my hands on the wide pine boards. That's when I can smell her; all that wetness. She lumbers toward me through the oiled dark, breathing hard, and all I can think is: I wonder how we'll look when they find us.

CASE 8

(April 2005)

EXHIBIT #2 *The woods are quiet*, Daria said. Yeah, what do you mean? *I mean they're quiet. No sound. No movement. Nothing. It's weird. It's like we're walking around in a photograph.* So we stood side by side for a moment, surveying the area. She held the sack of morel mushrooms, I the aluminum red trowel we ended up not needing. But my daughter was right. The woods *were* quiet. No chipmunks to scold us, no birdsong woven throughout the treetops. There was even an absence of mosquitoes to complain in our ears. The sunlight splashing between the pines seemed staged, as if part of a bigger set piece. *I think Chuck said there was a patch of apple trees this way*, Daria said. A patch, I asked. Since when do trees grow in patches? Daria smiled at me. *You're such a dork*, she said.

EXHIBIT #4 My breathing grew elevated, and I could feel a cool film on my neck, sweat blooming in knots on my T-shirt. We crested a hill, and I could make out two or three arthritic apple trees about 100 yards away. *How much do these things sell for again*, Daria asked. Like, thirty bucks a pound. *Oh. How much do we have now?* She stopped and opened her sack, looked in. I was suddenly reminded of when Daria was little, no older than nine. She was dressed as a Dalmatian that year. Her twin sister, Marie, was Cruella de Vil. She was mad because Marie kept stealing her Kit Kats. Marie had just started showing signs of getting sick that fall, but we were still months away from anything serious. No, I'm not! I'm not stealing, Marie yelled. *Yes you are, I saw you hide the wrappers!* Did not! *Did too, liar!* Girls, girls, I pleaded. You're a jerk, and Dad loves me more anyway, Marie said. Hey, I said, and immediately felt guilty because all three of us knew it was true.

EXHIBIT #6 The apple trees were old, beaten. Their low branches stretched out above the ground like diseased arms. I immediately noticed several morels near the base of the first tree; they looked like tiny, dusty brains. Bingo, I said. Daria tipped her head down and scooched under the branches. She began gently pulling the mushrooms up. Careful not to break them, I said. *Dad, please*, Daria complained. I heard two women whispering behind us and looked over my shoulder. I expected hikers. *What's wrong*, Daria asked, not looking up. I couldn't see anyone, and the voices stopped. Nothing, I said. Daria kept working. Did you hear that, I asked. *Hear what?* I listened. Everything was quiet. Nothing, I said again.

EXHIBIT #7 I weighed the sack in my hand. I think our work is done here, I said. Daria smiled. *Nice! Gonna make it rain*, she said and began sliding imaginary bills off her open palm. Let's go, I said. Our feet crunching the leaves and pine needles was the only sound for a while. As we made our way up the little hill, Daria began to hum a song behind me. It was a song Marie had asked for on the last day, lying there criss-crossed in tubes and wires, her head naked as a baby bird's. Sing it again, she said to me before closing her eyes. Sing it again, Papa. My wife and I held her hand, bewildered. Daria stayed in the bathroom the whole time, the door locked. What are you singing, I asked Daria now. *Oh, just some song*, she said.

EXHIBIT #9 When we got to the bottom of the hill, I couldn't tell if we'd been here before. I put my hands on my hips, looked around. *What's wrong*, Daria asked, a little winded. Um, did we come this way?

Daria looked left and right. *Of course. I think so. Why?* No, it's just... this doesn't look familiar, I said. Daria and I stood a moment longer. If there had been crickets, they're all we would have been able to hear. Instead, nothing but a dropping sun and shadows stretched mutely across soil and dead leaves. *The car's this way*, Daria said. *Don't be so dramatic.*

EXHIBIT #10 About fifteen minutes later, we heard a dog barking in the distance. We froze. Do you hear that, I asked. *Duh*, Daria said. The dog kept barking. And barking. It first sounded like it was in front of us, but then like it was to the left of us. *Do you think...* Shh! I said, holding my hand up. The dog continued barking another thirty seconds, then made a quick, high-pitched sound. Then the barking stopped. *What happened*, Daria asked. I cocked my head a bit. Strained. I don't know, I said. But let's get moving. It's getting dark.

EXHIBIT #15 When it became too dark to see, I used the light on my phone to guide us. The going was slow and both of us kept tripping, kept stumbling in the phone's half-light. *I still can't get a signal*, Daria said. She was looking at her phone and then holding it to her ear. Finally, my phone ran out of power. Daria's followed suit in a couple minutes. We stopped walking and huddled up close. *Dad, I'm scared*, Daria said. Before we all went downstairs to leave for Marie's funeral, Daria hid in her closet. My wife couldn't deal with much of anything, so I went into the closet to fetch her. She was sitting on the floor in the back. Hey, I said. Whatcha doing back there, sweetie? *This is what it's like to die*, Daria said. *All this darkness.* Oh, come on, that's not true, I said. Don't say that. I slid a row of little dresses out of the way. Daria looked up at me. *It's true*, she exclaimed. *Except when you die, there are others with you.* I squatted down and gripped Daria's thin shoulders. Sweetie... *Marie told me*, Daria said. *Marie says they won't stop touching her.*

EXHIBIT #17 After about a half hour of sitting down together, I ate a few of the morels. *How are they*, Daria asked. Raw, I said. The dark was so thick and so silent and so complete. Maybe we should sleep here, I finally said. *What? Are you nuts?* What else are we going to do? We can sleep until first light and then go and get help. *Help from where*, Daria demanded. I realized I had no idea. *Did you hear that*, Daria asked. Hear what, I said. *Is that someone talking?* I listened. Sweetheart, I don't hear anything. Daria found my hand. *Dad*, Daria asked. I shifted my weight. Yes? *Was Marie afraid to die?* Um, that was a long time ago. *Was she?* Maybe, I said. I think so, yes. *What was that*, Daria said. What was what, I asked. *That sound!* Daria, you need to just calm down, I said. And that's when I heard it. Behind me. The voice of a little girl I once knew, once loved above all others.

CASE 22

(July 2006)

EXHIBIT #3 The new house was magnificent—a Georgian five-bedroom with an endless backyard and wild apple trees deeper in the woods. Every morning my wife and I drank coffee as our yellow lab, Rusty, ran the perimeter unheeded. Why didn't we leave the city sooner? We smiled and sipped and laughed. We felt blessed.

EXHIBIT #8 Our only neighbor, a musician from a rock band famous in the 80s, heard I was a poet and something of an antique buff, so he invited me over to help him evaluate his first edition copy of *The Wizard of Oz*. The book suffered from a cracked spine, copious water stains, and some torn pages. *It's not worth a lot*, I told him. He shrugged his shoulders and smiled. The box that contained his book also held other items: a wooden toy train with a red chimney; a mummified sparrow; antique playing cards with flabby, naked women; and a small, hand-bound leather notebook, which he offered to me. For your poems, he said. I brought the book home and placed it on my nightstand and didn't think of it again for a week.

EXHIBIT #15 Yesterday, I needed to jot down an address and remembered the book. Beautifully crafted, the pages were thick, high-quality paper all unblemished and smooth—except for the last page. On the corner in careful blue script was what looked like a phone number. I googled the first three numbers, and they came back as the area code for San Antonio, Texas. I called the number. The phone rang many times but finally picked up. I heard a woman in the background yelling in Spanish, then silence. *Hello*, I said. *Hello?* Finally, a man cleared his throat into the receiver and licked his lips. *Hello*, I repeated. Cellar, the man said, and hung up. I called the number again, but no one answered.

EXHIBIT #16 I went over to my neighbor's house. The front door was open, and I could see him sitting at his piano, writing music. I told him about the number and the odd call. What did he say to you, he asked. I told him again. He invited me inside and took the box of items out from under the stairs. He told me he found them there after he moved in over a year ago. They belonged to the previous owner. *Who was the previous owner*, I asked. I don't know, the State auctioned this place, my neighbor said. All I know is that he lived alone and died in this house. They found his body in the cellar. My neighbor smiled at me. Awful, right?

EXHIBIT #17 *Redacted.*

EXHIBIT #18 I threw out the notebook at the town dump, along with an old brown suit I never wear. I watched the compactor crush and crumble its payload: a small white lampshade, an anonymous pizza box, two black trash bags popping like noxious bubbles. And there was a harder sound, like teeth breaking. The notebook sank below the mess and didn't resurface. I felt relieved.

EXHIBIT #21 When I got home, I found my wife in the living room reading. Her feet were propped up on the nineteenth-century ottoman I always told her not to prop her feet on. Our neighbor stopped by, she said. He seemed pissed. *Why*, I asked. He said if you didn't like his gesture you just should have told him. I didn't say anything. The notebook. If you didn't want it, you should have told him. Finding it on his pillow kind of creeped him out, you know? I felt bad and took the thing back.

Did you actually go into his house when he wasn't there? *Where's the book*, I asked. My wife tipped her head in the direction of the dining room. On the table. I went into the dining room. Rusty was on the large Moroccan rug. He sighed and thumped his tail when I entered. There, on the table, was the notebook. I didn't swallow or speak. I opened the pages. In the back was the original phone number in blue ink. Now underneath, in pencil, was mine.

CASE 34

(September 2013)

EXHIBIT #2 Zack attached the trail cam to a birch tree; he was sure feral hogs had taken to rooting through the compost and nearby garden but wanted proof. "There," Zack said. "Screw you, piggies." "Babe, how's it look," Janine called. "Not bad," Zack said as he stood back from the camera, hands on hips. He glanced back at his wife and son. Janine was tossing the Nerf to Mason, and every time he caught it he yelled, "Hotdog!" "Mason, it's touchdown, remember," Zack said. Janine made a face. "Come on, hon. He's five. Who cares?" Zack turned back to the camera, looked down the wooded path. The early September sun was thin and warm. They'd only been moved in for about a month and Zack thought if it wasn't one thing it was another. "Hotdog," Mason yelled again. "Okay," Zack said, turning slowly. "Who's ready to fight the Evil Bigfoot?" Zack raised his arms and laughed in a deep voice, running at his wife and son. They both screamed in unison, absolutely thrilled.

EXHIBIT #5 Janine sipped her tea in bed while reading an oversized World History book on her lap. "You know the Phoenicians were fucking rock stars, right?" Zack spit a mouthful of toothpaste into the white ceramic basin and looked back up at the mirror. "The Phoenicians?" "Yeah," Janine called. "Their boats and navigation skills were out of bounds." "Out of bounds? Who are you, Guy Fieri," Zack asked as he came out of their bathroom and slipped under the covers. Zack leaned into Janine's body, kissed her neck. She smelled like lavender and honey. "You're lucky I don't *look* like Guy Fieri," Janine said, flipping a page over. "Fat chance," Zack said. He moved in closer. "Come on, Mason's still awake," Janine said without looking at him. Zack was about to protest when they heard someone run through the yard.

EXHIBIT #6 Janine pointed the flashlight from the doorway, her bathrobe shut tight with the other hand. She directed the beam toward Zack and the garden. She could see his own light moving back and forth across the grass. "See anything," she asked. Zack didn't respond. "Zack," she called. "Hey, Zack." "Shh, you'll wake the neighbors," Janine heard him say. "It's cold out here," she said. "Well, go inside." She looked across the street at the Timley's house. Mr. Timley was looking back through his living room bay window. Oh, for God's sake, Janine thought and cinched her bathrobe tighter. "Zack," Janine said. "I'm going in." "Wait," Zack said. "You gotta be kidding me," he said to the darkness.

EXHIBIT #8 Janine held Zack's hand under the faucet in the kitchen. Zack grimaced. "It's not a big deal," he said. Blood splashed with the water and ran pink down the drain. "It could get infected," Janine said. Zack made a face again, took his hand back. "It's fine." Janine sighed, tore off a wad of paper towels. "Well, here then. Try not to bleed all over the house." Zack pressed the paper towels against his hand. "I'm sorry," he said. "I'm just a little freaked out." "It's gonna need stitches," Janine said. Zack removed the paper towels; a deep, three-inch slice ran cleanly across his palm. "Probably," he said. "But whatever." "How did you do that again," Janine asked. "I really don't know. As I got closer to the camera, I leaned down a little, putting my hand against the tree. Then I slid my hand up, and *bam*!" "Maybe you caught it on one of the bungee hooks or something," Janine said. She moved in to get a closer look. "Yeah, maybe." "Is Daddy okay?" Janine let out a little sound, and Zack flinched. Behind them, Mason stood in the kitchen doorway in his racecar pajamas. "Mason, sweetie, you startled us," Janine said, smiling.

"Yes, Daddy just got a little boo-boo." Janine went around Zack and picked Mason up. "I had a dream you got hurt," Mason said. "You did, buddy," Zack asked. Mason put his head on Janine's shoulder. "Yeah, you were outside in the yard. A little man was hiding behind our trees, so you couldn't see his teeth. He kept hurting you. Mommy was crying because she knew it would be her turn next." Zack tried to look calm. "Shhh-shhh-shhh. That's just a bad dream, sweetie." Zack rubbed Mason's head. Janine's eyes were wide, but Zack wouldn't look at her and just concentrated on Mason. He rubbed his son's smooth face and blond hair until Mason began to breathe steadily. And the three of them were quiet then, huddled in the kitchen light.

EXHIBIT #11 *Redacted.*

EXHIBIT #12 Zack called his office and said he'd be out for the day; Mason woke up with a slight fever and needed to stay home from kindergarten. Mason's temp had only been 99.5, but rules nowadays said any sign of a fever and you needed to keep your child home. You should have seen how it was when I was a kid, Zack thought. Unless I was pissing blood, I was forced to go to school. But Zack didn't mind. Janine had a full schedule and his hand was killing him anyway. Besides, he wanted to see if there were any photos on the trail cam. Mason sat on the living room floor with a bowl of green grapes and watched *Little Einsteins*. He'll be okay by himself for a couple minutes, Zack thought, and quietly slipped out the side door and into the backyard.

EXHIBIT #13 The sky was blue and deep as a lake. Zack popped the memory card out of the bottom of the trail cam and back into the Canon SureShot. He looked back and forth for any sign of movement in the woods, briefly searched the ground for any hoof prints. Nothing. He powered the camera on while walking into the house, and the photo counter said the total had risen from 101 to 106. Aha, Zack thought as he made his way inside and sat at the dining room table. I got you. Zack could hear the Little Einsteins singing about adagios in the living room. "How you doing, little man," he said. "Good," Mason said. Zack looked at the camera's flat screen and fast- forwarded past old shots of Mason's fifth birthday, the trip last winter to New Orleans, and this year's Easter egg hunt at the old house. Mason looked cute with his white bunny ears, proudly hoisting the full wicker basket above his shoulders. That's when Zack landed on the first photo from last night. The picture was a night vision shot of the compost pile in its chicken wire hoop, the side of a pine tree, and the beat-up tool shed in the background. Wholly unremarkable. The second photo was the same. And the third. Zack could feel his excitement deflating. But the fourth plainly showed the snout, ears, and bristled backside of a wild hog standing next to the chicken wire. Zack sat up. "Damn," he said out loud. "There you are." The thing was at least four feet long and all black. He thought he could also see little tusks. Jesus, it's a bona fide razorback, he thought. Zack was thinking about the next steps, if he'd need to capture the beast, or worse, shoot it. What if it came into the yard? Even during the day? What if it tried to gore Janine or Mason? Zack pictured his son's little body flying into the air and the terrible sounds the pig would make as it bit into the soft flesh of Mason's face and neck. The fifth photo made Zack blink, sure he was seeing it wrong. It still showed the wild pig standing next to the compost, but now there was a little hand reaching from outside the frame and touching the back of the hog. It seemed to be resting on the animal, almost steadying it. The hand looked about the same size as Mason's. "Hey Mason," Zack could hear himself say out loud. "Can I ask you a question?"

EXHIBIT #16 Mason kept saying no every time Zack found a new way to ask him if he woke up last night and went outside for any reason. "Are you sure, little man? I won't be mad." "No," Mason replied, looking up at the ceiling, exasperated. "I just came downstairs when I heard you and mommy fighting." "Hey, we weren't fighting," Zack said. Zack noticed Mason's face had grown increasingly flushed and reached out to touch his son's forehead. "Mason, are you feeling hotter, sweetie?" "Kinda,"

Mason replied. Zack looked his son in the eyes; the whites had an almost blue tint to them—a sure sign of dehydration. Zack picked Mason up and carried him upstairs to his room. Mason grew limp in Zack's arms, radiating heat through his pajamas like a tiny skeleton of fire.

EXHIBIT #17 Mason was sweating even though Zack pressed a cold cloth against his forehead. He'd already had his boy drink some Children's Advil and wash it down with several cold sips of Gatorade. The thermometer started beeping, and Zack took it out of Mason's mouth: 103 degrees. "Shit," Zack said. "Mommy said no swearing," Mason said, and Zack smiled. He had already texted Janine, and she was on her way home. "Let's get these pj's off," Zack said. Mason just kind of rolled around as Zack got his shirt off. The heat radiating from his body reminded Zack of morning-after campfires. He moved the cloth across Mason's torso, his thin arms, felt the cloth grow warm in his hand. "Does this house scare you," Mason asked. Zack stopped. "What," he said. "This house," Mason repeated. "What are you talking about," Zack said. Mason smiled, and his teeth were bright. "Listen sweetie, you need to rest, okay? You have a fever and…" "He told me you'd get yours, Daddy. That we all would." Zack blinked, licked his lips. "Who did?" "He's in the kitchen," Mason said. That's when Zack heard the breakfast table and chairs stutter across the linoleum, as if someone were sitting down to eat.

EXHIBIT #18 "Hello," Zack yelled as he slowly made his way down the stairs. He was clutching a coat hanger, the closest thing he'd found to grab. "Hello," he said again. Zack smelled what he thought were black truffles; that funky, animal sweat kind of smell they had, and he stopped. The smell was raw, alive. Zack gagged, put the back of his hand to his mouth. He thought his heart was going to pound out of his chest. "Whoever you are, I called the cops, and they're on the way," Zack lied. "So you better just leave." He inched his way through the dining room and heard Janine's car pulling up in the driveway. Zack stepped into the kitchen.

EXHIBIT #20 Janine got out of her car and walked toward the side door. Dr. Willis had said he'd make room in his schedule, and they could bring Mason in right away. She hoped Zack was ready to go and glanced up at Mason's window. The curtain fluttered as Mason stepped out of view. Janine stopped. What the hell, she thought. She moved urgently to the door and opened it, stepping inside the mudroom. "Zack," she called. She hung her car keys up on the little hook. "Why is Mason..." "In here, Mommy," Mason said from the kitchen. He sounded happy, and Janine felt relieved. She walked into the kitchen. All the chairs were splayed, and it looked like Zack was on the floor behind the table. He was making small, wet noises. Janine opened her mouth. "Now it's your turn, Mommy," Mason said.

CASE 56

(June 2018)

EXHIBIT #3 My wife Lisa and I thought we'd never finish moving into our new home, but after the final boxes were emptied, I thought: Just get the lawnmower stowed away and it's time to crack the champagne. I jogged the mower down to an old shed in the backyard and popped the little deadbolt on the door. Inside was bare, save for a wool blanket draped over something against the aluminum wall. Underneath, I discovered a hand-carved headboard and footboard. The craftsmanship was striking, and the mahogany pieces were clearly very old. In the headboard was what looked like a purple thistle chain, carved delicately around the edges—when I ran my thumb across the carvings, it gave me the same pleasure as touching a letterpress book. Later, I asked Lisa about it. Oh, Suzanne and what's-his-name left that when they moved out. She said they had no more room. I guess it came with her great-grandmother, over from Scotland or whatever. *Why the hell would they leave behind something so valuable?* Lisa shrugged. Beats me.

EXHIBIT #5 That night, my neighbor Walter asked me over for a glass of Armagnac. We'd met last month while the realtor was giving Lisa and me a tour of the property. He told me he was widowed some years ago, and I figured the guy was lonely. *How well did you know Suzanne?* I asked. Walter sipped his drink. She was a friend. *Oh. Do you know about* *her headboard in the shed?* She left that here? *Yeah, and the footboard too. Actually, it's the whole frame.* Can I look at it? he asked.

EXHIBIT #6 Inside the shed, we trained our flashlights as I made the grand reveal. Beautiful, Walter said. Did you see the names, he asked. *What names?* We pulled the headboard clear of the blanket and turned it around. Carved on the bottom left corner were four names: *Abigail, Claire, Violet,* and *Jocelyn.* They were sisters, all distant cousins of Suzanne. I guess their parents were real pioneer folk back then. Indians got 'em, Walter said.

EXHIBIT #9 It was well after midnight. Lisa was on top of me, eyes closed. She moved her hips with increasing urgency; the mahogany frame carried us like a ship, matching us rhythm for rhythm. That's when I heard the whispering, several voices at once. I opened my eyes and Lisa cried out, gripping my shoulders tighter. *Wait,* I said. Lisa moved faster, and the frame groaned in our wake. *Wait,* I said again and slid from underneath her. What the hell are you doing? she said. *Listen!* The air was humid and still. Crickets vibrated outside the open window, and the moon glowed silver against the sill. My wife's chest heaved as she caught her breath. I don't hear anything, she said. I strained and turned my head to one side. *I heard voices,* I said. You heard what? *People talking.* Lisa slipped under the covers. Is someone outside the window? I got up and looked. The plum trees shook in a new breeze. I turned and glanced under the bed. Nothing. Come back to bed, Lisa said. You scared me.

EXHIBIT #12 Walter refilled my glass. That's bizarre, he said. Are you sure? I swirled the snifter beneath my nose: caramel and apple. *I think so. I don't know. It was so surreal.* And it was clearly voices? Like whispering? *Yes,* I said. What were they whispering about? I shook my head. *I guess it could have been kids or something, messing with us.* You know, Walter said, Judy down the street has four kids. Little pests. They're always getting into trouble. Fucking welfare family. I arched an eyebrow, surprised.

I looked out the window, I said. *No one was there. And I had just assembled Suzanne's old bedframe in our room.* Why would you do that, Walter said. *Do what? Use the bedframe? Why not*, I said. *It's beautiful. And we own it now, so....* You don't own it, Walter said. You found it.

EXHIBIT #17 The basement smelled like heating oil and damp earth. I was rummaging through a plastic tub for screws but couldn't find the right size. A truck or large van sounded like it was pulling up in our driveway. Hope that's Amazon, I thought and turned to peek out the small window at ground level. Behind a stack of Mason jars, a tiny mouse skittered and ran. *Shit*, I yelped, backing up. The mouse darted behind a large red cabinet, unhinged from the stone wall. Babe, what the hell was that, Lisa said from the top of the stairs. *Oh, I saw a mouse down here, and it freaked me out. Sorry.* No, my wife said. What was the loud noise? It sounded like something was rolling. Lisa came down a few steps. I looked up at her in the dim throw of a bare bulb. *Rolling? That was probably the truck I heard. Did you check the driveway?* It didn't sound like it was coming from the driveway. *Where was it coming from*, I asked. It sounded like it was coming from upstairs, she said.

EXHIBIT #22 The faucet was running in the bathroom, Lisa brushing her teeth. I stood in my boxers, staring at the bed. The frame was dark; the light purple of the carved-in thistle added a nice contrast to our white comforter. A bard owl sounded his call through the open window, mapping the distance between us and him. I smiled. Everything is fine, I thought. Everyone just relax. Whatcha doing, Lisa said from right behind me. *Jesus!* I looked over my shoulder, startled. Goodness, you're jumpy. *No, I'm just thinking.* Well, don't think too hard, you're bound to pull something. Lisa smiled and moved around me, flipped back the comforter, and got in bed. *Always the funny guy*, I said.

EXHIBIT #24 I woke with a start, feeling as if I was late or had forgotten something. My wrists felt itchy, irritated. I looked down. In the early morning light, I could see raised bumps and scratches circling both wrists. I was silent, my mouth open; I turned my hands and wrists back and forth, amazed. *Sweetie,* I said. Lisa didn't move. I nudged her hip. *Sweetheart, you have to wake up and see this.* I looked down at my wife. She slowly rolled over. Her face was puffy and covered in scratches, tiny red slits and bumps. Her eyes were swollen shut. I could barely recognize her. When she opened her mouth, her lips cracked and exposed dried blood in between. Her hands found her face. She made a sound, thick and throaty. My face! *No, no, it's okay, it's okay,* I said. My face! It hurts.... She was crying, the tears all backed up around her encrusted, sealed eyelids. I pulled her up to me as she shook and sobbed a terrible, muffled sound.

EXHIBIT #25 The emergency doctor gave Lisa Benadryl and prednisone, some kind of pain med. He asked if we owned a cat or if either of us ever sleepwalked. I said no to both. The nurse cleaned and washed my wife's face. The swelling went down. She could open her eyes. I kissed her cheek and told her we were going home soon. While waiting to sign discharge papers, the doctor asked to speak with me privately outside the room. I remembered my wrists and put my hands in my pockets. During the night, did you get up? Get a snack or go to the bathroom? *No.* Do you think your wife got up and went outside, maybe didn't want to tell you? *Why would she do that?* I asked. No reason. Look, I'm just trying to help you figure out why your wife looks like she fell face-first into a rosebush. While perfectly asleep.

EXHIBIT #28 During the ride home, we didn't talk much. Lisa kept touching her face, kept looking in the visor mirror. It's going to scar, she said. I occasionally looked over at her but mostly stared into the long pull of black asphalt before me. I realized I was gripping the wheel too tight; my knuckles shined like moons. I asked Lisa what she wanted for dinner. She didn't respond. *You know, I can order some Thai, or...* I don't want to sleep in that bed anymore, Lisa said.

EXHIBIT #30 I made Lisa mint tea and got her settled on the couch. She wrapped herself in a blue blanket, turned on *Oprah*. I told her I was going to Walter's for a quick minute. I found him outback sitting at his patio table. He was looking at photos of Suzanne, the previous owner of my house. He was crying. I love her, he said. I love her so much. She promised me she was leaving her husband. She lied to me. Embarrassed, I told him I was sorry. He smiled and kind of laughed, wiped his face. *I'm putting the bed frame back in the shed. I might actually burn it,* I said. My neighbor didn't blink, only shook his head. Suzanne didn't have the heart to destroy it, he said. She told me she dropped it off at the dump. Guess she lied about that too. I watched a robin hop across the grass, stab at a worm. You should definitely burn it, Walter said.

EXHIBIT #31 I went back inside my house and closed the door. I could hear Oprah saying that weight loss was a personal journey. *Honey,* I said from the kitchen. I walked into the living room. The blue blanket was on the floor. Everyone on *Oprah* began clapping. *Honey,* I said again, louder. I heard a thump above me in the bedroom. I stared up at the ceiling. I navigated quickly through the living room and up the stairs. Our bedroom door was closed. I could hear my wife grunting on the other side. I knocked on the door while opening it. *Babe?* The room was empty. I stared at the neatly made bed. THEY'RE TRYING TO GET IN, my wife bawled from somewhere out of sight. I flinched, stepped back. HELP ME! GET THE GIRLS! She was screaming from under the bed. I dropped down on my knees and flicked the comforter up. Lisa was on her back, clawing at the frame above. Her face was spattered with what looked like blood, and her eyes were filled with horror. WHERE ARE THE GIRLS? she bellowed. *No, no, no,* I said. *Oh my God, NO!* I scuttled under the bed frame to try and get her. I could smell prairie grass and cook fires. I could hear noises of women screaming and a thunder of horse hooves. Hold the door with me, she said breathlessly. They're trying to get in. Don't let those savages take our girls. I looked up at the frame and pushed. I could hear high voices yelling and a commotion of bodies on the other side. The frame shook and pounded. Someone was chopping. The frame began to splinter. Lisa was sobbing. A harder blow hit, and I saw the curved end of an axe break through, inches above my face. I could smell sweat, could hear a language I didn't know, but I could tell it was happy, victorious—and then the axe came down again.

Acknowledgments

I would like to thank the editors of the following magazines where some of these stories first appeared:

Barrelhouse
Flash Fiction Magazine
SmokeLong Quarterly

and the Authors League Fund, for much needed financial assistance during the completion of this book.

Photo: © Sophie Locke

Christopher Locke's writing has appeared in such magazines as *The North American Review*, *The Rumpus*, *SmokeLong Quarterly*, *The Sun*, *Poetry East*, *Verse Daily*, *Southwest Review*, *Slice*, *The Literary Review*, *West Branch*, *Gargoyle*, *The Nervous Breakdown*, and *Saranac Review*, as well as on NPR's Morning Edition and Ireland's Radio One. Locke's most recent book is *Ordinary Gods* (Salmon Poetry, 2017), a collection of poems & essays detailing his twenty-five years of travel throughout Latin America, and his first post-punk/spoken word album, *Late Lights*, was recently released by Burst & Bloom Records. Locke has received over a dozen grants, fellowships, and awards for his writing including the Dorothy Sargent Rosenberg Poetry Award, state grants from the Massachusetts Cultural Council and the New Hampshire State Council on the Arts, and Poetry Fellowships from Fundacion Valparaiso (Spain) and PARMA (Mexico). He teaches creative writing online at The Poetry Barn and in person at North Country Community College in the Adirondacks.